Full Court Fever

For Clark —

Hoop it up!

Fred Bowen

Books by Fred Bowen
T.J.'s Secret Pitch
The Golden Glove
The Kid Coach
Playoff Dreams
Winners Take All
On the Line
Off the Rim
The Final Cut
Full Court Fever

JR

<u>A Peachtree Junior Publication</u>
Published by
Peachtree Publishers, Ltd.
1700 Chattahoochee Avenue
Atlanta, Georgia 30318

Text © 1998 by Fred Bowen
Illustrations © 1998 by Ann G. Barrow

Jacket illustration by Ann G. Barrow
Book design by Loraine M. Balcsik
Composition by Dana Celentano

Manufactured in the United States of America
10 9 8 7 6 5 4

Library of Congress Cataloging-in-Publication Data
Bowen, Fred.
    Full court fever / Fred Bowen : illustrated by Ann Barrow. —1st ed.
       p. cm. —(Allstar sportstory)
       Summary: With help from a new student and inspiration from an old magazine article, the players on Michael's seventh-grade basketball team hope to overcome their shortness and win their game against the eighth graders.
       ISBN 1-56145-160-6
       [1. Basketball—Fiction.] I. Barrow, Ann, ill. II. Title. III. Series: Bowen, Fred. Allstar sportstory.
PZ7.B6724Fu 1998   97-35294
[Fic]—dc21   CIP
                                                                           AC

Full Court Fever

by Fred Bowen

Illustrated by
Ann Barrow

PEACHTREE
ATLANTA

For my parents,
for my brothers and sisters,
and for all the house championships,
lost and won,
at 42 Leicester Road.

ONE

Michael Mancino could hear the game as he approached the park next to the school. He heard the ball pounding the pavement and sneakers scraping against the blacktop. He heard voices rising into the sunlit winter sky and the distant clanging of a loose metal rim.

After Michael turned the corner of the tan brick school building, he stood for a moment with his basketball on his hip and studied the court in front of him.

He saw Kelvin Wells, Conor Kilgore, and Charlie Rosenthal, three of his teammates from the Falcons seventh-grade basketball team, shooting baskets. Their breath and voices sent small puffs of white mist into the chilled December air.

Suddenly the ball bounced wildly off the court. Charlie jogged after it, looked up, and saw Michael standing at the side of the school.

"Hey, Michael's here!" he shouted. "Now

"Michael stood for a moment with his basketball on his hip and studied the court in front of him."

we've got enough for a game of two-on-two."

Michael trotted onto the court, took a few quick dribbles with his basketball, and attempted a long shot. Air ball.

"How about Michael and me against you two?" Conor suggested, ignoring Michael's shot.

Kelvin and Charlie eyed each other in silence. "I don't know," Kelvin said slowly.

"Come on," Conor said, sounding annoyed. "We're all about the same size. Let's just play."

"Hey, let me have a couple of shots, will ya?" Michael said, grabbing the boys' basketball and dribbling around the court. "You guys are all warmed up."

But Conor was ready to play. "Well, hurry up," he said impatiently.

"Game to seven. We'll switch teams after each game," Kelvin said.

"All right," Conor agreed.

"I'll shoot to see who gets the ball first," said Kelvin, placing his feet at the foul line. He bounced the ball three times and eyed the rim.

"Hey, can we play?" a voice sounded from the other end of the court. The four friends turned and squinted into the setting sun. There, standing like a tall picket fence, were four eighth graders: Jake McClure, James Becker, Jerome

Dobson, and Johnny Palotta. The four boys walked closer, their long shadows stretching black across the court.

"Uh-oh," Charlie whispered to Michael. "It's 'The Four Js': Jake, James—"

"Jerome and Johnny," Michael chimed in, finishing the lineup.

"We're just starting a game," Kelvin said to the newcomers, and he turned to look back at the basket.

"Come on, let's play four-on-four," James Becker said, dribbling closer to Kelvin and his teammates.

The seventh-grade Falcons looked at each other, agreeing in silence.

"Okay, what are the teams?" Conor asked.

"Us four against you four," James said with a wide smile.

"No way!" Michael blurted out. "You guys are all eighth graders."

"Yeah," Kelvin agreed. "You're all older and taller than we are. You'll kill us."

"Come on, you guys are just a year behind us," Jerome Dobson said, flipping an easy jump shot at the basket.

"All right," Michael said. "The four eighth graders against the four seventh graders. But Kelvin shoots to see who gets the ball first."

Kelvin set his feet once again across the foul line. He bounced the ball three times and took a deep breath, then dipped his legs slightly and sent the ball spinning toward the basket. *Swish.* Nothing but net.

Jake McClure grabbed the bouncing ball and tossed it to Michael. "Your ball," he said. "Game to eleven by ones. I'm covering Michael."

The boys darted into action. Michael snapped a quick pass to Kelvin, who passed to Conor for the shot. *Swish.*

"1–0," Michael said happily. "Winners out, right? If a team scores a basket they keep the ball, right?"

"Winners out," Jake agreed.

Michael passed to Charlie in the corner. Charlie faked a shot, then dribbled underneath the basket and spun a shot against the backboard and through the net.

"All right. 2–0!"

"My man, Charlie!"

Then Kelvin made a long jump shot and the score was 3–0. "Are we playing 7–0 is a shut-out?" Kelvin asked with a grin.

Jerome Dobson bounced Kelvin the ball. "You're a long way from a shutout, wise guy. Just play ball."

Kelvin's next jumper bounced off the rim, and James Becker got the rebound. "Let's go to work," he cried.

The older boys did just that. Using crisp passes and their greater height, the eighth graders worked the ball close to the basket for easy scores. In no time, the younger Falcons lead had vanished and the eighth graders were ahead.

"What's the count?" Michael asked, catching his breath.

"6–3, us," Johnny Palotta replied.

"Come on, let's get some rebounds," Conor pleaded.

Michael darted out and intercepted the ball, whirled quickly, and flipped a pass to Charlie. Charlie swished a short jumper. 6–4.

But that was the last basket Michael and his friends could score. The eighth graders scored five straight baskets. James Becker muscled up over Charlie, sending Charlie's glasses flying as he scored the final basket.

"Game," James said as the ball fell through the net. "Do you guys want to play another?"

"No, thanks," Charlie said, leaning over to pick up his glasses.

"Come on, guys," James said to his friends. "Maybe we can find a real game up at the high school."

The older players strutted off. "See you boys at the end of the season," Johnny called back over his shoulder.

"Yeah, good luck in the seventh grade–eighth grade game," Jerome said.

Michael and his friends milled around the basket, tossing up lazy shots.

"How are your glasses, Charlie?" Michael asked.

Charlie tilted his glasses. "They're kinda wobbly, but that's okay," he said. "Do you guys want to play two-on-two?"

"Nah," Kelvin said, shaking his head.

"Man, they killed us," Conor said.

"We had it going for a while," Charlie said bravely. "We were up 3–0."

"Yeah, but we lost 11–4," Michael said flatly.

Kelvin took a shot. "It's the same old problem," he said. "We got no big guys, so we get no rebounds."

"We're not really small," Michael said. "We're just regular."

Kelvin laughed. "So we get beat regular."

"We're fast, and we're good shooters," Michael insisted. "We hardly missed a shot."

"Yeah," Kelvin agreed as the boys each started to head for home. "But before you can shoot the ball, you gotta *get* the ball."

TWO

Michael dribbled all the way home. First he dribbled with his right hand. Then he switched and dribbled with his left. Always keeping his head up, Michael moved easily through the streets of his hometown.

As he turned the corner onto his street, Michael could see the basketball backboard and rim nailed to the Mancinos' garage exactly ten feet above the blacktop driveway.

Michael's father had set up the basket shortly before Michael's parents had divorced. That was five years ago.

Good, Mom's car isn't here. I can practice my jump shot, Michael thought as he dribbled up to the house and noticed the empty driveway. He pulled off his sweatshirt and tossed it on the muddy lawn. Then he took a quick dribble and shot a long jumper that bounced off the rim. He reached up, grabbing the ball as fiercely as he would in a real game.

"Mancino snaps down the rebound," Michael said, pretending to be both the announcer and the player in a professional game. "He dribbles to the corner. The defense just can't stop him. He shoots." Michael lofted a perfect jump shot that floated up to the basket and splashed through the net. He threw his hands up in celebration and shouted: "Mancino scores! It's all over. The Falcons win!" He tried to make his voice sound like the roar of 10,000 screaming fans.

"Hey, Michael Jordan. You know when Mom's getting home?"

Michael felt the blood rush to his face as he turned and saw his older brother Daniel standing in the back doorway. "I think she's trying to sell the Schafer house," Michael said, trying to act as if his face weren't bright red. "She'll be back for dinner. Where have you been?"

"Working at the House of Cards. Hey, a guy brought in a whole bunch of old *Sports Illustrated*s today. There must be over two hundred. They're cool. Where have you been?"

"Down at the park. I was playing hoops," Michael said, practicing his between-the-legs dribble.

"Who was there?"

"Some of the guys from the team: Kelvin,

Conor, and Charlie. We played a bunch of eighth graders."

"How'd you do?"

"They killed us, 11–4. We couldn't get any rebounds," Michael said with a frown, remembering the game.

"You gotta keep moving around against those big guys," Daniel said, trying to offer some advice.

"We *were* moving. But that didn't do any good!" Michael snapped back. "Those guys are gonna kill us in the seventh–eighth grade game at the end of the season."

Daniel nodded. "The eighth graders always win that one. They're older and bigger."

"Yeah, I guess."

Daniel stepped out onto the driveway and held out his hands for the ball. "Come on," he said, "give me a shot."

Michael passed the ball to Daniel, who banked a quick jump shot through the net.

"One-on-one for the house championship," Daniel suggested, tossing the ball to his brother.

Michael groaned. "Man, if I can't beat an eighth grader, how am I gonna beat a tenth grader?"

Daniel's face twisted into a look of disgust.

"You're never gonna beat me if you just keep whining about it," he said. "Come on. Game to seven. Your ball."

Michael sighed, sensing his second defeat of the day. "Okay," he said.

On the first play, Michael faked and drove hard to the right. He hooked a shot up over Daniel's outstretched hand, and the ball nudged off the backboard and through the hoop.

"Lucky shot," Daniel said, tossing the ball to Michael.

Next Michael tried a quick shot that bounced off the rim. Daniel grabbed the rebound and dribbled back to the foul line. He backed his way to the basket, bumping his younger brother closer to the hoop. Then he tossed in an easy ten-foot jumper.

"1–1," Daniel said cheerfully.

The game continued, hard fought like the thousand house-championship games before. Michael used his speed and skill to try to overcome Daniel's size and strength.

"What's the count?" Michael asked after scoring on a twisting layup.

"6–4," Daniel answered. "My way."

"Gotta win by two?" Michael asked.

"Daniel snatched the rebound, dribbled to the foul line, and whirled around, driving hard to the basket."

Daniel shook his head. "Nah. Straight seven. It's getting dark. First guy to seven wins."

Just then, the boys' mom pulled the family car into the driveway and honked the horn.

Michael and Daniel waved her back.

"Don't pull the car up, Mom," Daniel said. "We're almost done with the game."

Janine Mancino stuck her head out the car window. "You kids want to go out for pizza tonight? I sold the Schafer house."

"Yeah, one second. Just one more basket," Daniel answered. "I gotta teach Michael some respect for his older brother."

Michael dribbled right, then spun quickly to his left. But Daniel reacted quickly and forced Michael to take an off-balance shot. The ball clanged off the rim. Daniel snatched the rebound, dribbled to the foul line, and whirled around, driving hard to the basket. Michael dashed back on defense, trying to block his brother's path to the basket. But Daniel placed the ball high above Michael's hands and laid in the winning basket.

"Game. 7–4," Daniel said, patting Michael on the head. "Maybe next time, little brother." Michael stared up at the rim and then turned to watch his older brother run to the car and get into the front seat.

"Come on, Michael, hurry up," his mother called.

Michael picked up the ball and tossed one last shot through the strings. Then he walked slowly to the car and got in the back seat.

THREE

"All right, warm-up drill. Chest passes," Coach Cummings called.

The seventh-grade Falcons eagerly lined up in the four corners of the basketball court.

"Go!"

Michael started dribbling as fast as he could. Looking up, he snapped a chest pass to Gina Brillante, who was standing in the middle of the court. Gina was a high school junior who was Coach Cummings's assistant coach. Gina returned the pass to Michael, who caught it, dribbled, and passed to T. J. Burns at the opposite end of the gym. T. J. raced by Michael, who got in line behind Kelvin. Soon two lines of flashing Falcons were streaking up and down the court through the rays of afternoon sunlight that slanted in from the windows high above the polished gym floor. The two coaches shouted instructions above the echoes of squeaking sneakers and pounding basketballs.

"Head up, T. J. Always look up."

"Come on, Conor. Let's hustle."

"Snap passes, Kelvin. Nothing sloppy."

"Stretch it out, Bobby. You're running like a duck."

"Left hand, Michael, left hand."

Coach Cummings's whistle pierced the noise of the gym.

"Layups," he called.

Without a word, the Falcons broke into two lines. Passes flew. Players ran. A steady stream of balls glanced off the glass backboard and into the net. Again the whistle sounded.

"All right, line up along the foul line by height," Coach Cummings ordered. "T. J. to my left, tallest guy to my right."

The Falcons fell in line, finally settling on an order after several good-natured arguments.

"There's no way you're taller."

"I got you by an inch, Conor."

"I'm taller than you, Bobby, you just got taller hair."

Coach Cummings, a tall young man with a whistle dangling from his neck, stood in front of the Falcons and smiled. "There's our problem," he said. "You guys are all about the same size."

"Except T. J.," Kelvin said, laughing. "He's the smallest."

"The only thing big about you, Kelvin, is your mouth," T. J. shot back.

"Cut it out," Coach Cummings said sternly. "Well, we don't have any big guys so we better learn to rebound. Come on, Gina. Let's show 'em."

The coaches stepped toward the basket.

"Listen up," Coach Cummings called. "We might have won our first game if we had gotten more rebounds."

The team crowded closer, and the coach tossed the ball to Charlie Rosenthal.

"Take a shot, Charlie. Gina, you go for the rebound and I'll keep you from getting it: I'll box you out."

As the ball left Charlie's hands and floated toward the basket, the coach described what he was doing. "When the ball goes up, I start boxing out Gina. That means that while I'm looking for the rebound, I'm keeping Gina behind me. I'm blocking her so she can't get the rebound before I do."

Charlie's shot bounced high off the rim, and Coach Cummings kept talking. "Okay, now I keep my eye on the ball, and Gina's behind me. She's trying to get around me but I get my

18

"Charlie's shot bounced high off the rim, and Coach Cummings kept talking. 'Okay, now I keep my eye on the ball, and Gina's behind me.'"

hands up, jump, and reach for the rebound."

Coach Cummings leaped and pulled the ball from the air, letting out a loud "Aargh!" His booming voice filled the gym.

The Falcons laughed as the coach landed with a thud.

"You guys think it's funny," he said with a smile. "But rebounding is attitude. You gotta be aggressive to be a good rebounder. So I want to hear some roars."

The coach tossed the ball to Charlie. "Take another shot," he said. "Gina, try to get around me."

Again the ball went up. "Remember, keep your feet moving. Stay between your man and the basket," Coach Cummings said.

Another leap. Another roar. Another rebound.

The coach rested the ball on his hip. "If we do it right," he said, "we can get rebounds even without big guys."

Coach Cummings pointed to the basket at the other end of the floor. "Gina, you take T. J., Conor, Bobby, Danny, and Jason down there. Michael, Kelvin, Martin, Walter, and Charlie, stay with me."

"Okay," Coach Cummings said to the five players gathered around him. "One player shoots. Two players box out the other two players for the rebound. Any questions?"

Coach Cummings looked at the Falcons. "Okay. Let's go, and I want to hear some roars."

Michael and Kelvin stood under the basket ready to box out their teammates, Martin Estevao and Walter Albee. As Coach Cummings watched, Charlie tossed up a jump shot. Michael and Kelvin battled to hold their positions, their sneakers squeaking against the polished floor. The ball bounced off the rim and backboard toward Kelvin's side of the basket. Kelvin quickly moved in front of Walter and set his feet for the rebound. As he leaped, Kelvin gave out an enormous roar.

"Aargh!"

But the ball bounced off Kelvin's fingers and trickled out of bounds.

Coach Cummings couldn't keep from laughing. "You've got the roar down, Kelvin," he said. "Now let's try to get the ball."

An hour later, after practice, Michael stood under the same basket, grabbing rebounds and tossing the ball out to Gina, who flipped shot after shot up to the basket. Kelvin sat with his back against the padded gym wall, his practice shirt dark with sweat and his legs stretched out in front of him.

"Come on, Kelvin," Michael scolded. "I thought you were gonna help me rebound for Gina."

Kelvin let out a deep breath. "Man, I'm tired from all that roaring."

"You laugh," Gina said as she swished another shot, "but if you do what the coach says, we'll get some rebounds and win some games."

"Yeah, maybe," Kelvin answered. "But it sure would be a lot easier on my voice if we just had some big guys."

FOUR

"Come on, guys, box out. We gotta get some rebounds!" Coach Cummings yelled, standing above the huddle of Falcons during the time-out. Michael looked past his circle of team-mates at the scoreboard. The Woodlin Wizards were up by six points.

Looks like we're gonna lose another one, Michael thought, shaking his head.

"There's plenty of time left." Coach Cummings took a deep breath and sounded calmer than before. "T. J., report in for Walter."

The referee's whistle blew. Coach Cummings put his hand out into the middle of the huddle. Michael put his hand on top of the coach's hand, and the players' hands piled up, one on top of another. "Let's box out and get some rebounds!" Coach Cummings said firmly.

"DEE-fense!" the Falcons shouted as they yanked their hands from the pile and headed back onto the court.

The Wizards stretched the lead to 33–25 on a quick basket. But the Falcons came back when Conor hit a long jumper. 33–27.

Then Michael darted out and picked off a careless crosscourt pass. He dribbled in alone for an easy layup. 33–29. The Wizards missed their next shot and Kelvin grabbed the rebound with a roar. He passed the ball to Michael, who saw T. J. racing downcourt. Michael's pass was perfect, and T. J. laid the ball in to make the score 33–31.

The Wizards coach was up off the bench. "Time out. Time out!" he called.

The Falcons bench was on its feet too.

"Good hoop, T. J."

"Great pass, Michael."

"How to roar, Kelvin."

The time-out seemed to settle the Wizards. They came downcourt and worked the ball in to their tallest player with a series of quick passes. Keeping the ball high, the tall player turned to the basket and shot the ball over Charlie Rosenthal.

Michael heard a hard slap against the tall Wizard's wrist as the ball left his hand and headed for the basket. The referee's whistle blew as the ball rolled around the rim, touched off the backboard, and fell through the net.

"The basket is good," the referee said. Then he pointed to Charlie. "Foul on number 22. One shot," he said.

The Wizards foul shot hit the back of the rim and bounced long. Michael reached high for the rebound, but a taller Wizard forward snapped down the ball.

Michael looked desperately at the scoreboard. Wizards 35, Falcons 31. *Down by four, their ball, and only a minute and a half left to play,* he thought. *We gotta get the ball back.* Coach Cummings stood at the Falcons bench waving his arms. "Pick up men!" he shouted, ordering the Falcons to play man-to-man defense.

The Falcons shouted out the players they were covering.

"I got number twelve."

"Michael, take the blond guy."

"T. J., cover number six."

But in the confusion, the player Michael was supposed to be covering suddenly cut to the basket, caught a bullet pass, and laid the ball in. Michael's shoulders sank. *Man, I never should have let that guy score!* Michael thought. The Falcons were down 37–31 with less than a minute to play.

The game seemed to drift away after that. The teams traded baskets, but the Falcons chances for victory had vanished.

After the game, Michael walked over to the scorer's table where his brother Daniel was working as the official scorekeeper.

"Good game," Daniel said. "You guys almost came back in the fourth quarter."

"Almost," Michael said. His voice was tired and discouraged.

The two boys studied the scorer's sheet.

POS	PL D NUM	PLAYER NAME	FOULS	FIRST HALF SCORING	SECOND HALF SCORING	1ST	2ND	REBOUNDS	ASSISTS	POINTS	
G		Mancino		2 1	2 2			11	11	7	
G		Burns		2					1	2	
C		Rosenthal	1		2			卅		3	
F		Kilgore		2 2 1 1	2 2			11	1	10	
F		Crammer			3			1		3	
F		Wells	2					1	1	2	
C		Estevao			2			11		2	
F		Black	2					11		2	
G		Li			1				1	1	
G		Albee			1			11		1	
		TEAM TOTALS		14	19			17	6	33	

OFFICIAL SCORER Daniel Mancino
OFFICIAL TIMEKEEPER

TEAM Falcons   COACH Cummings   DATE 1-11   REFEREE C. Pink
PLAYED AT ____ RECORD W____ L____   GAME NO. ____   REFEREE ____

	1ST QUARTER	2ND QUARTER	3RD QUARTER	4TH QUARTER	OVERTIME	OVERTIME	FINAL SCORE
H	9	14	21	33			33
V	9	18	26	37			37

Daniel circled a number on the sheet.

"You guys didn't get many rebounds," he observed. "You gotta box out."

"We *were* boxing out," Michael protested. "They just reached over us."

Michael's mother joined the two boys and put her arm around her younger son.

"That was a great game," she said. "You really played hard."

Michael smiled a weak smile.

"You ready to go home?" his mother asked.

"Sure."

As the Mancinos drove through town, Michael sat in the back seat staring out the window at the lightly falling snow and the passing Christmas lights. Daniel and his mother sat in the front seat talking about the holiday, but Michael wasn't listening. He was still thinking about the game.

"Oh!" his mother exclaimed. "Let's go by the town Christmas tree."

Janine Mancino drove the family car carefully through the town's narrow streets. The snow crunched beneath the tires as the Mancinos pulled to a stop in front of the small park where the tree stood tall and bright.

The family stood together under the tree

and watched as the colored lights playfully twinkled on and off.

"Do you remember when you boys were little and I brought you down here to see Santa Claus?"

"Sure," Daniel laughed. "Michael was so scared, he burst into tears."

"Of course I was scared," Michael said, remembering. "He was huge!"

The boys inched closer to their mother, leaning against her for warmth from the biting cold. For a few moments, no one said anything. They were happy just to be looking up at the tree and breathing in the scent of fresh evergreen.

"What are you boys wishing for this Christmas?" Michael's mother finally asked.

Michael kept looking up into the falling snow, the dark green tree, and the multicolored lights. He knew just what he wanted for Christmas.

I wish the team could get a big guy, he thought.

FIVE

On the first day back from Christmas vacation, Michael and Kelvin stood studying the basketball schedule posted on the wall outside the gym.

7th Grade Boys Basketball

Dec 14	1:00 P.M.	at St. Johns	L 35–30
Dec 21	4:00 P.M.	Woodlin	L 39–33
Jan 11	2:00 P.M.	at Eastern	
Jan 18	4:00 P.M.	at Burtonsville	
Jan 25	1:00 P.M.	Rock Creek Valley	
Feb 1	3:00 P.M.	Strathmore	
Feb 8	1:00 P.M.	at Cresthaven	
Feb 15	4:00 P.M.	Riverdale	
Feb 22	3:00 P.M.	at Bell	

* *

| Mar 1 | 2:00 P.M. | 7th Grade Boys vs. 8th Grade Boys | |

"Looking at the schedule won't change the scores," Theresa Scott said, sneaking up behind her classmates. "You guys will still be 0–2."

Michael sighed. "We've got seven games to turn the season around," he said, sounding determined.

"Yeah, before we get waxed by the eighth graders," Kelvin said, pointing at another schedule on the wall. "Look, they're 2–0."

"We can beat them," Michael said.

"At what?" Kelvin laughed.

Just then, Conor, Charlie, and T. J. came running down the hall.

"Have you seen him?" Conor asked breathlessly. Charlie and T. J. stood wide-eyed beside him.

"Who?" Michael asked.

"The new kid," Charlie said.

"What about the new kid?" Kelvin asked.

"He's huge!" Conor blurted out. "He's gotta be six feet, easy."

"He's head and shoulders above me," T. J. said.

"So what?" Theresa laughed. "*I'm* head and shoulders above you, T. J."

"Where's he from?" Michael asked.

"Nigeria," Conor answered.

Michael and Kelvin looked at each other and knew they were thinking the same thing.

"Hakeem Olajuwon!" they shouted, trading high fives. "Hakeem the Dream."

"Oh, that's right!" Theresa exclaimed. "Olajuwon is from Nigeria, too. And he's one of the best big players in professional basketball!"

The bell rang for first period. Michael and Kelvin almost danced down the hall to math class.

After everybody took their seats, the new student came in, his large frame swallowing up most of the doorway. He handed a note to the teacher, Mr. Petty.

Kelvin leaned over and whispered to Michael, "It's him. And look, he's taller than Mr. Petty!"

The new student spoke briefly with Mr. Petty, then walked down the row and squeezed into an empty desk next to Michael. His knees bumped against the bottom of the desk.

Michael smiled. "Hi," he said. "I'm Michael Mancino."

"Hello," the new student answered. "I am Dikembe Obiku."

"All right, class. Let's get started," Mr. Petty said from the front of the room.

Michael opened his book. "Hey," he whispered to Dikembe. "Do you play ball?"

"Yes." Dikembe smiled. "I like to play ball," he said slowly and carefully.

"Really, what position?" Michael asked, becoming more excited.

*"Kelvin leaned over and whispered to Michael, 'It's him.
And look, he's taller than Mr. Petty!'"*

"I like to play forward."

"Gee, I thought you would be a center."

"Yes," Dikembe said, smiling and nodding. "Center. Forward."

"Mr. Mancino," Mr. Petty interrupted. "Would you take the next problem?"

Michael's eyes moved swiftly back to his book. "Yeah...sure," he faltered. "Uh...I kinda lost my place...what problem are we on?"

"If you were paying attention, you would know," Mr. Petty said sternly. "Problem three."

The class continued but Michael just couldn't keep his mind on math. He kept looking over at Dikembe. The new boy sat up straight at his desk, his posture making him appear even taller. The pencil he held seemed tiny in his large hands.

Man, look at those hands, Michael thought. *This guy will be a great rebounder. He's just what the team needs.*

After class, Michael asked Dikembe, "Do you know where your next class is?"

"Physical Education," Dikembe answered, studying a computer printout of his class schedule.

"That's our next class too," Kelvin said.

"Yeah, come on," Michael said, already halfway

out the door. "We'll introduce you to Coach Cummings."

When they got to the gym, the three boys walked straight to the coach.

Michael talked so quickly that his words almost tumbled over each other. "Coach, this is Dikembe. He's a new seventh grader from Nigeria. You know, like Hakeem Olajuwon. He plays center and forward."

"Yes." Dikembe nodded. "Center. Forward."

"Really?" Coach Cummings asked, suddenly interested. "Well, let's see what you can do."

Coach Cummings tossed Dikembe a basketball as Michael and Kelvin stood off to the side, twitching with excitement.

"Let's see you dribble, Dikembe," Coach Cummings said.

"Dribble?" Dikembe asked, looking down at the basketball in his hands.

"You know, bounce the ball up and down," the coach said, motioning with his hand.

Dikembe began to dribble, slapping at the ball awkwardly.

Michael shrugged. "He's a big guy," he whispered to Kelvin. "He doesn't have to handle the ball that well."

"Okay, let's see you shoot," Coach Cummings

said, flipping a perfect jump shot through the hoop. He nodded to Dikembe.

Dikembe bent at the knees almost mechanically and pushed his basketball toward the basket. The ball smacked against the backboard with a loud *thwack* that caused Michael and Kelvin's heads to snap back with surprise.

"Did you play much basketball in Nigeria, Dikembe?" Coach Cummings asked gently.

"No, I play football."

"Football?" Michael cried with dismay.

"Yes. No...not American football. I play what you call soccer."

"I thought you said you played center and forward," Michael said, feeling his dream slip away.

"Yes, I play center-forward," Dikembe said proudly. "I score many goals."

Michael and Kelvin groaned. Coach Cummings put a friendly arm on Dikembe's shoulder. "If you would like to learn some basketball, you can come to our practices."

Dikembe nodded agreeably. "I would like to learn basketball."

"I can't put you on the team. But—hey, I know," Coach Cummings said, stumbling upon an idea. "Dikembe, maybe you could be the team's manager. That way you could meet some friends, help out at practice, and learn some basketball. What do you think, guys?"

Michael and Kelvin did not answer. They still could not believe that Dikembe only played soccer.

"I would like that." Dikembe smiled. He walked away, practicing his dribbling as he went.

Coach Cummings turned to Michael and Kelvin, almost laughing. "I don't think he's going to be Hakeem the Dream. At least not this year. I guess you guys will just have to learn to rebound."

SIX

Michael, Kelvin, and Conor walked swiftly through the town. Their hands were thrust deep into their coat pockets, their shoulders hunched tight against the cold. The snow, ice, and sand crunched under their heavy boots.

"Where are we going?" Kelvin asked. "I'm freezing."

"The House of Cards, that sports shop where my brother Daniel works," Michael answered.

"Why are we going there?" Conor asked.

"My Uncle Dave gave me a $15 gift certificate there for Christmas," Michael explained.

"What are you gonna get?"

"I don't know." Michael shrugged.

The three boys entered the store, the cold winter wind whisking in behind them. Michael waved at Daniel, who was working behind a counter filled with sports cards and other collectors' items.

"Hey, you could get a Ken Griffey Jr. card,"

Conor said, pointing at a display case.

"Yeah, but I'd blow the whole fifteen bucks on one card," Michael said, shaking his head.

"How about a Frank Thomas or a Cal Ripken?" Conor persisted.

"Nah," said Michael, moving toward the back of the small store. "I don't know if I want to get a card. I've got lots of them."

In a back corner, Michael discovered what he was looking for. "Hey," he called to his friends. "Here are the old *Sports Illustrated*s Daniel told me about. They look pretty cool."

Conor and Kelvin made their way to the back of the store. The boys stood at the racks, leafing through the old magazines.

"Man, these things are really old," Kelvin said. "Here's one from 1963."

"How much are they?" Michael asked.

"Five bucks," Conor answered.

"Wow, they used to be a quarter," Michael said, looking at a cover.

"Man, look at this one," Kelvin laughed, holding up a magazine and reading aloud. "December 9, 1963. 'Smart Moves that Score Points.' Look at these guys," he said, showing off a magazine with two basketball players drawn on the cover. "They don't even look like basketball players."

"Can you believe those shoes?" Conor laughed, pointing at the magazine cover. "They look more like slippers than basketball shoes."

Kelvin looked through the magazine. "The magazine predicts the top twenty in college basketball for the 1963–64 season. Guess what school they picked for Number One."

"North Carolina?"

"Nope."

"Kentucky?"

Kelvin shook his head.

"Kansas?"

"Nope. NYU," Kelvin said.

"Who?"

"New York University," Kelvin explained. "The Violets."

Michael pulled the magazine out of Kelvin's hands. "No way!" Michael exclaimed. "NYU doesn't even have a team anymore."

Daniel came up in back of the three boys. "Hey, guys, cut it out," he warned. "If you rip a magazine, Mr. Mondore will make you buy it."

"Hey, Daniel, who won the NCAA basketball championship in 1964?" Michael asked, still looking at the top twenty.

"How should I know? I'm 15, not 50." Daniel grabbed a thick book off the shelf and handed it to Michael. "Look it up in this sports almanac."

"What exactly is the NCAA, anyway?" Conor asked.

"That's the big tournament for college teams," Michael said, looking down a long column of school names in the sports almanac.

"Oh yeah, I knew that," said Conor.

"Hey, the UCLA Bruins won in 1964," Michael said. "What does the article say about them, Kelvin?"

"They aren't even in the top twenty," Kelvin said. "Here they are. Listen to this." Kelvin began to read slowly. " 'Except for guard Fred Goss, who has quit to concentrate on studies, the whole Bruin team that won its conference last year is back. UCLA could repeat, but its lack of height again will make things tough.' "

Kelvin laughed. " 'Lack of height'! The UCLA Bruins sound like our team!"

"Yeah, but they won the NCAA tournament that year. How did they do that?" Michael wondered out loud.

"Probably found a big guy," Kelvin said with a shrug.

"Hey, here's another magazine about college basketball," Conor said, holding up a *Sports Illustrated* issue and reading. "March 29, 1965.

'How UCLA Won Again.'"

"Let me see," Michael said, pulling the magazine away from Conor and reading. "It says here that UCLA won the NCAA Championship for the second straight year. They beat Michigan even though the Michigan players were a lot taller."

"Really? How'd they do that?" Conor asked.

Michael kept reading. "It says UCLA used a full-court zone press the whole game and just out-quicked them," Michael explained. "There's a diagram of the full-court press printed in the magazine."

Conor and Kelvin stood behind Michael. The three friends studied the diagram. They looked at each other, the same thought bubbling up in their minds.

Kelvin shook his head. "It won't work," he said.

"Why not?" Michael asked. "We're all small and quick just like the UCLA Bruins."

"If it's so great, why don't teams use it now?" Kelvin asked, almost daring Michael to answer.

"Lots of teams press, just not all the time," Michael explained.

"Wait a minute," Conor said, eyeing another issue on the rack and pointing to the cover.

"The three friends studied the diagram, the same thought bubbling up in their minds."

"December 6, 1965," Conor read. "'The UCLA Press: How to Beat It.'"

Michael snapped the *Sports Illustrated* issue out of the rack and placed it with the two others in his hand.

"I'm getting all three of these magazines," he said, marching up to the cash register.

"What are you gonna do with them?" Kelvin asked as he and Conor followed.

"You'll see," Michael said over his shoulder.

SEVEN

The next afternoon, a group of six boys stood on the cold, barren blacktop of the Hobbs Park basketball court.

"Come on, Michael, let's get going," Kelvin complained. "We're freezing our butts off."

"Okay, okay. I'm expecting more kids to show up. They're just a little late," Michael said to the boys. They stood in their winter coats and gloves, rubbing their hands together and shuffling their feet to stay warm.

"I thought you said Bobby, Danny, and Walter couldn't make it," T. J. said, clapping his gloved hands together in the cold. "How are we gonna get more players?"

"You didn't ask the eighth graders, did you?" Kelvin asked.

Michael shook his head. "I don't want them to know."

"Know what?" Martin asked.

"You'll see."

Just then, Dikembe and three girls, Theresa Scott, Nikki Lawrence, and Eliza Helyar, rounded the corner of the school. All of them were dressed in brightly colored parkas and hats, and Dikembe's bright red hat bobbed along far above the others.

"Here are our players," Michael said, smiling and dribbling toward the school. "Thanks for coming."

Theresa smiled back. "Anything to help you guys finally win a game."

"What gives, Michael?" Kelvin asked. "What are we doing out here?"

"I thought you played basketball inside," Dikembe said, sounding a bit confused.

"We can only play inside when the team has the gym for practice," Michael explained. "So we've got to play here, okay?" He reached into his jacket, pulled out some papers, and gave one to each of the boys on his team.

"Hey, this is that *Sports Illustrated* page that shows the UCLA full-court press," Conor said, looking down at the copy he held in his gloved hands.

"What about us?" Theresa asked. "How about giving us a copy?"

"You three girls and Dikembe will try to beat

the press," Michael said.

Dikembe stood off to the side kicking the basketball between his feet like a soccer ball. "You want me to play?" he asked, a bit surprised.

"You bet," Michael answered. "But we want you to play basketball."

"I am not very good yet, but I have been practicing," Dikembe said with a smile.

"Hey, wait a second, Michael. There are only four of us and six of you," Nikki observed. "That's not fair."

"And so what if we can stop them with the press? That doesn't prove anything," Kelvin argued. "Will it work against real ballplayers?"

"What do you mean, *real* ballplayers?" Theresa protested. "At least we've *won* our two games."

"How's this," Conor suggested. "We'll give you Kelvin."

"Yeah, Kelvin." T. J. smiled. "If you don't think the press will work, let's see you beat it."

Michael held up his hands. "Come on, I didn't bring everyone down here to fight," he said. "Let's take our coats off and get to work."

"Take our coats off!" Kelvin yelped, as though in pain. "No way. I'm freezing with mine on!"

The other kids put their coats, gloves, and scarves in a pile on the frozen earth at the edge of the court. Michael huddled with his teammates. Pointing to his paper, he called out instructions. "The idea of the press is that we play defense all over the court and drive the other team crazy."

Michael's teammates stared intently at the diagram and Michael kept talking. "When the other team has the ball, *two* of our players cover the guy with the ball and force him to pass. Our three other players then move in and try to intercept the pass. That's the full-court press."

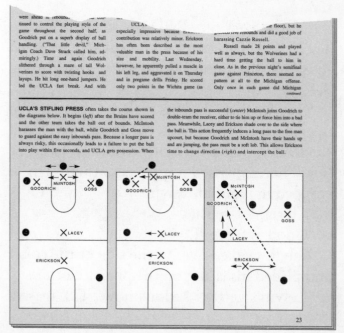

were ahead in rebound... ...and continued to control the playing style of the
game throughout the second half, as
Goodrich put on a superb display of ball
handling. ("That little devil," Michigan Coach Dave Strack called him, ad-
miringly.) Time and again Goodrich
slithered through a maze of tall Wolverines to score with twisting hooks and
layups. He hit long one-hand jumpers. He
led the UCLA fast break. And with

UCLA'... ...especially impressive because Erick...
contribution was relatively minor. Erickson
has often been described as the most
valuable man in the press because of his
size and mobility. Last Wednesday,
however, he apparently pulled a muscle in
his left leg, and aggravated it on Thursday
and in pregame drills Friday. He scored
only two points in the Wichita game (as

...e floor), but he
...ged five rebounds and did a good job of
harassing Cazzie Russell.

Russell made 28 points and played
well as always, but the Wolverines had a
hard time getting the ball to him in
close. As in the previous night's semifinal
game against Princeton, there seemed no
pattern at all to the Michigan offense.
Only once in each game did Michigan
continued

UCLA'S STIFLING PRESS often takes the course shown in the diagrams below. It begins (*left*) after the Bruins have scored and the other team takes the ball out of bounds. McIntosh harasses the man with the ball, while Goodrich and Goss move to guard against the easy inbounds pass. Because a longer pass is always risky, this occasionally leads to a failure to put the ball into play within five seconds, and UCLA gets possession. When the inbounds pass is successful (*center*) McIntosh joins Goodrich to double-team the receiver, either to tie him up or force him into a bad pass. Meanwhile, Lacey and Erickson shade over to the side where the ball is. This action frequently induces a long pass to the free man upcourt, but because Goodrich and McIntosh have their hands up and are jumping, the pass must be a soft lob. This allows Erickson time to change direction (*right*) and intercept the ball.

23

47

"Sounds cool," Conor said, and the others nodded their heads. "What positions should we play in the press?"

Michael pointed at the names of the UCLA players on the diagram

"T. J., Martin, and I will be Goodrich, McIntosh, and Goss, the three guys at the top of the press. Charlie, you play Lacey, the man in the middle. And Conor, you play back like Erickson."

Michael looked around. The Falcons seemed ready. "Okay," he said, clapping his hands. "Let's try it."

On the first play, Nikki passed the ball to Theresa. Michael and T. J. immediately pounced like cats, surrounding her with a swarming defense.

"Downcourt!" Kelvin yelled. "Theresa, I'm open." But when Theresa tried to pass, T. J. and Michael waved their arms wildly in front of her. Theresa tossed a high pass that Charlie stopped in front of Kelvin.

"All right, Charlie."

"Good defense, T. J."

Kelvin walked over to the side of the court and placed his jacket on the pile of clothes.

"Kelvin's getting serious now," T. J. teased. "Watch out!"

This time Nikki passed to Kelvin, who was quickly surrounded by two defenders.

"Move!" Kelvin shouted, looking around the court. Finally he lofted a long, desperate pass toward Dikembe. But Conor leaped up and intercepted it.

Kelvin looked at Michael. A small smile passed like a shadow over Kelvin's face. "This may be trickier than I thought," Kelvin admitted.

The game continued as the team worked out the secrets of the UCLA full-court press. After more than an hour, the kids quit playing and started to put on their winter jackets.

"You do not have to let the other players dribble down the court, do you?" Dikembe asked.

"Right." Michael nodded. "With the full-court press we try to steal the ball before the other team shoots, instead of always trying to get rebounds after they shoot."

"I like that." Dikembe smiled. "That is more like soccer."

Michael turned to the others. "What do you think about the press?"

"I think it's cool," said Conor. "I just wish we had time to show it to Coach Cummings in a practice before our next game."

"'Move!' Kelvin shouted, looking around the court."

"Yeah, it's working. We should keep practicing it," T. J. agreed. "I never get any rebounds anyway."

Theresa laughed. "The press might actually help you guys win a game," she said.

Finally, the group turned to Kelvin.

"What do you think, Kelvin?" Michael asked.

Kelvin eyed the group and smiled. "I still think I'm freezing my butt off," he said.

EIGHT

Phweeet! The referee's whistle blew just as the ball left Michael's hand.

"Foul. Green. Number 14. On the arm." The referee signaled as he spoke. "Two shots."

The horn at the scorer's table sounded. The scorekeeper waved his arms and called, "The quarter is over." The referee nodded and declared, "The foul occurred before the buzzer. White ball, two."

Michael stayed at the foul line as the teams left the court. He glanced up at the scoreboard: Eastern was ahead by ten.

"Two shots," the referee repeated as he handed Michael the ball.

Michael set his feet at the foul line and

bounced the ball three times. *Use your legs and follow through,* he reminded himself. He shot. *Swish.* The first shot was good. But the second shot fell short and Michael was kicking himself as he joined the Falcons huddle around Coach Cummings. *We're gonna need every single point if we're gonna come back,* Michael thought.

"All right. We're down nine, but we still have eight minutes to play," Coach Cummings said, trying to rally the team. "We gotta play good defense and take good shots."

"Who's playing the fourth quarter?" Martin asked.

Coach Cummings looked around the huddle. "Let's have Charlie, Conor, and Michael up front," he decided. "T. J. and Martin in the backcourt."

Coach Cummings reached his hand into the team's circle and all the hands piled on top of his. "Let's try to get some rebounds," he said wearily.

"DEE-fense!" the Falcons shouted in unison. The five fourth-quarter players jogged onto the court.

Michael called them into a huddle in the middle of the floor. "Come on, guys, we can do it," he implored.

Conor looked around the huddle. "You know, Michael, we're down by nine. Since we're the five guys who practiced the UCLA press, why don't we try it?"

Michael shrugged. "You want to?" he asked his teammates.

The Falcons nodded.

"Yeah, let's do it," Martin said firmly. "We have nothing to lose."

"Okay," Michael said, leaning into the huddle. "We'll press any time we score a basket. I'll yell 'Bruin' to remind us."

"Why 'Bruin'?" Conor asked.

"For the UCLA Bruins," Michael said.

"White ball," the referee called to begin the final quarter.

The Falcons got off to a quick start. T. J. passed to Michael in the corner, who faked left, drove right, and canned a quick jump shot.

"Bruin!"

Instantly, the Falcons set up the press. Their shouts and squeaking sneakers echoed in the gym. Michael waved his hands wildly in front of the Eastern player trying to pass the ball inbounds.

Surprised, the Eastern player tried a bounce pass toward the corner. Martin stepped in front and stole the ball. Now on offense, Martin flipped a quick pass to Charlie, who was calling for the ball. Charlie tossed a high jump shot that dropped through the net. The score was 31–26.

"Bruin!" yelled Michael.

This time the Eastern player tried a long pass. But Conor alertly jumped in front and intercepted. Conor dribbled downcourt, faked a shot, and passed to Martin for an easy layup.

The Eastern coach was on his feet.

"Time out!" he yelled, his hands forming the letter *T*.

The Falcon bench was on its feet and fired up.

"Great play, Conor."

"Way to go, Martin."

But Coach Cummings looked confused. "What are you guys doing?" he asked.

"It's the UCLA full-court press," Michael explained, a bit out of breath.

"Yeah...but...but..." Coach Cummings stammered.

"Looks like it's working, Coach," Gina said. "We're only down three. 31–28."

The Falcons looked at their coach and waited.

"Come on, Coach," Conor pleaded. "Like Gina said, it's working."

"Okay, okay," Coach Cummings decided. "Since it's working, let's stay with it. Remember, keep hustling."

On the next possession, an Eastern player dribbled past the first three Falcons in his path. But Martin kept hustling and tipped the ball loose from behind. Charlie grabbed the ball and tossed a pass to Michael, who dribbled in for an easy layup.

"Bruin!"

The press continued to work its magic no matter what the Eastern team tried and no matter which Falcons were in the game. The speedy Falcons turned Eastern passes into loose balls, loose balls into interceptions, and interceptions into Falcon baskets. The Falcons had pulled ahead, 41–35.

At the end of the game, Martin dribbled out the final seconds as the Falcon bench shouted the countdown: "Three...two...one!"

Coach Cummings stood on the sidelines with his hands on his hips and a slightly puzzled look on his face. The happy Falcons came off the court and formed a celebration huddle.

"Well, Coach, what do you think of the press?" Michael asked.

Coach Cummings paused as if he were still collecting his thoughts, then broke into a smile.

"I think it will be even better after we practice it."

NINE

Michael hurried down the school hall.

"No running in the corridors," Mr. Petty called above the noise of voices and slamming lockers.

Michael saw a familiar head towering above a clump of students. "Hey, Dikembe," he called. "Are you going to practice?"

Dikembe turned and smiled. "You bet. I want to see you practice your new play."

Michael and Dikembe fell in step together. Michael had to double his pace to keep up with Dikembe's long stride. "How are the basketball drills that Coach Cummings told you about coming along?" Michael asked.

"They are okay," Dikembe answered with another smile. "I am learning to dribble with my hands. But I still wish I could use my feet."

Minutes later, Michael and his Falcon teammates were running their warm-up drills in the gym. The Falcons seemed happier and more up-beat now that they had a victory behind them.

They were feeling so confident that they could tease each other and no one's feelings got hurt.

"You call that a pass, Conor? That is so lame!"

"We're running, not jogging, Kelvin."

Following layups, Coach Cummings blew his whistle.

"Sit down on the stands, guys," the coach said. "Get the chalkboard, Gina."

Gina rolled over a large blackboard filled with basketball formations and set it in front of the stands.

Coach Cummings picked up a piece of chalk and said, "I've decided that we should play the full-court press all of the time."

The team eyed each other as they squirmed on the wooden benches. Coach Cummings continued and began drawing arrows on the blackboard across the formations as he spoke. "The idea of the press is to speed up the game," he said. "When a guy on the other team gets the ball, I want two Falcons on him. Don't let him get anywhere. Make him pass."

"We're gonna play defense on the whole court?" Bobby asked in disbelief.

"All 94 feet," Coach Cummings said firmly. He kept talking and drawing. "We'll force the other team to make long passes that we can intercept and turn into easy baskets."

Conor raised his hand. "What if the other team gets by the press, Coach?" he asked.

"We'll have to hustle back," the coach answered. "We can get lots of steals by sneaking up in back of the dribbler and knocking the ball loose."

"Aren't we gonna get awful tired pressing the whole game?" Kelvin asked, his tongue dangling out comically.

"Sure." Coach Cummings smiled. "That's why we're gonna need all the guys on the team to be in top condition and ready to play."

The coach paused and looked into the faces of his Falcons. "John Wooden, the great coach at UCLA who used this press years ago, said that three things are important for success in basketball: physical condition, fundamentals, and working together as a team." The Falcons nodded their heads in unison. "If we're in better condition than the other team, they'll get tired a lot sooner than we will. And the press will work much better."

Coach Cummings glanced at Kelvin. "Don't worry. If you or anybody else gets tired, just signal the bench by bending over and pulling at the bottom of your basketball shorts. Gina or I will see you and get you out of there. Okay?"

The coach clapped his hands and shouted, "We're not getting in good condition by sitting here talking; let's play ball!"

The Falcons bounded off the wooden stands with shouts and clapping hands. They were ready to go full court.

TEN

Michael stood along the foul lane waiting for the Burtonsville Bengals player to shoot his two foul shots.

Michael's heart pounded. His lungs burned from the wild, full-court fury of the game. *I really don't want to come out of the game,* Michael thought, *but I'm too tired to do the team any good right now.*

Taking a deep breath, he leaned over and tugged at the edge of his basketball shorts.

The buzzer sounded. Michael looked up and saw his teammate Walter Albee at the scorer's table pointing at him. Michael slapped hands along the bench.

"Good hustle," Gina said, grabbing Michael and pointing to the basket. "Remember, look up and use the bounce pass to get it in to Charlie in the middle."

Michael nodded and took a seat on the bench between T. J. and Dikembe. Then

Michael looked at the scoreboard as he gulped down some water. Down by three points.

"These guys are tough," Michael whispered to T. J. "The press isn't bothering them much."

"They're getting tired," T. J. said confidently.

Michael hung his head and stared at the floor. *So am I,* he thought.

When Michael looked up, he saw the Bengals point guard dribble around the pressing Falcons as the last seconds of the third quarter ticked away. Outside the three-point line, the Bengals guard stopped and let fly a long jump shot. The ball banked off the backboard and in just before the buzzer went off.

Three points! The Falcons trailed 37–31. Coach Cummings shouted above the noisy Falcons huddle as the team prepared for the fourth and final quarter. "Stay with the press, guys! You're wearing them down. We just need a couple of turnovers. Let's not let that kid get another lucky shot."

The Falcons put their hands into the huddle. "DEE-fense!" they yelled.

The final quarter started with the teams trading baskets. Conor and Bobby sank long jumpers to keep the Falcons close, 41–35.

"Good shooting, guys!" Michael shouted from the bench. "Comeback time!"

Michael leaned forward and looked down the bench to Coach Cummings. *Come on, Coach,* he thought, *put me back in. I'm ready.*

Moments later, Coach Cummings waved his hand toward the end of the bench and called, "Michael, go in for Bobby. Remember, keep the pressure on."

On the next Falcon possession, Martin passed to Michael on the right. Facing the basket, Michael faked a shot and bounced the ball in to Charlie, who laid it up and in.

Phweeeeeeettttttt!

"Foul. Red. Number 12. The basket is good. One shot," the referee said, signaling.

Charlie's foul shot rolled around the rim and in to make the score 41–38.

Michael shouted "Bruin!" He stepped in front of a Bengals player and intercepted the inbound pass. He turned and shot a quick jumper.

Swish! The Falcons now trailed by just one point, 41–40.

"Bruin!"

This time the Bengals point guard dribbled by the pressing Falcons. But Michael hustled back and tipped the ball loose. A crush of bodies scrambled across the floor, diving and scraping for the loose ball. Conor grabbed the ball out of the tangle and tossed a pass to Michael. Looking down the court, Michael whipped a perfect pass to Walter, who scored on the easy layup.

"Time out!" the Bengals coach shouted.

The Falcons bench was shouting too.

"Great hustle, Conor."

"My main man, Michael."

"Turn up the press!"

Coach Cummings held up his hands. "The game's not over, guys," he warned his celebrating team. "We're only up by one, 42–41, and there are almost two minutes to go." The coach pointed at Kelvin and said, "Kelvin is in for Walter. Let's keep the pressure on!"

The Falcons almost flew back onto the court. The Burtonsville Bengals came back onto the court more slowly and quietly. As the Bengals set up to pass the ball in, Michael could sense that the press had worked its magic. The

*"The Falcons were only up by one point
with almost two minutes to go."*

Falcons were waving their arms, moving their feet, and shouting. The Bengals seemed tired and defeated. The Falcons were only up by one point with almost two minutes to go, but Michael knew in his heart that the game was over. *They're done,* Michael thought, *we got 'em.*

Sure enough, two steals, two baskets, two free throws, and two minutes later, the Falcons were really celebrating. Their voices echoed in the Burtonsville school hall as they shouted all the way to the locker room.

"48–41! Big win!"

"Let's go, Falcons!"

"Don't mess with the press!"

Coach Cummings entered the locker room with a smile as big as a basketball.

"What do you think of the press now, Coach?" Michael asked.

"It's getting better every game," Coach Cummings said.

ELEVEN

Several weeks later, after five more games, ten more practices, and four inches of snow, Michael, Kelvin, Conor, and Dikembe stood outside the entrance to the gymnasium studying the seventh-grade boys basketball schedule.

7th Grade Boys Basketball

Dec 14	1:00 P.M.	at St. Johns	L	35–30
Dec 21	4:00 P.M.	Woodlin	L	39–33
Jan 11	2:00 P.M.	at Eastern	W	41–35
Jan 18	4:00 P.M.	at Burtonsville	W	48–41
Jan 25	1:00 P.M.	Rock Creek Valley	W	48–29
Feb 1	3:00 P.M.	at Strathmore	W	51–35
Feb 8	1:00 P.M.	at Cresthaven	L	44–42
Feb 15	4:00 P.M.	Riverdale	W	41–38
Feb 22	3:00 P.M.	at Bell	W	53–29

* *

| Mar 1 | 2:00 P.M. | 7th Grade Boys vs. 8th Grade Boys | | |

"Once we started pressing full court, we started scoring a lot more," Conor observed, tapping the schedule.

"And winning a lot more," Michael added.

"Yeah, but we couldn't beat Cresthaven," Kelvin said, slouching against the wall. "And anyway, that's against seventh graders. Check out what the eighth-grade team did against eighth graders. They were 7–2."

"They lost by ten to Burtonsville," Michael noted.

"So what?" Kelvin exclaimed. "Burtonsville's got that kid Bonner. He's huge. He can practically jam it."

"I'm big," Dikembe said from above the group. "That does not mean I'm good."

"That's different," Kelvin said. "You're just starting. And anyway, you're getting better every day."

"Hey, did you hear that Coach Cummings is going to let Dikembe play for a few minutes in the game tomorrow?" Michael announced, smiling.

"But how can Dikembe play?" Kelvin asked. "He's not on the team. He's just the manager."

"The game is between the seventh- and eighth-grade boys," Michael reminded him. "Coach Cummings usually plays the regular team, but he doesn't have to. He can play any seventh grader he wants."

Michael turned to his tall friend and asked, "Are you ready to show us what you got?"

A sad look crossed Dikembe's face. "I don't know if I will be able to play tomorrow," he said.

"What? Why not?" Michael asked.

"My uncle from Nigeria is coming in and my family is having a party."

"Yeah, but..." Michael started, disappointed.

"My mother says that family is more important than basketball."

"Mothers always say things like that, but this isn't just any game," Michael explained. "This is the seventh graders against the eighth graders."

"Don't worry, your press will beat the eighth graders."

Kelvin waved a hand at his two friends. "Fat chance," he said. "Every one of their starters is bigger than we are."

"So what?" Michael said, beginning to get angry. "Remember that NCAA Championship game between UCLA and Michigan? All of Michigan's starters were bigger than UCLA's and UCLA still won, 91–80."

"They're not just bigger, they're older. Heck, half their team is shaving!"

"We're playing basketball, not going to the barbershop!" Michael shouted, throwing up his hands.

"All I'm saying is that the seventh grade never beats the eighth grade!" Kelvin shouted back.

"The girls did once," said Theresa, standing in her uniform in back of the boys with a basketball on her hip.

"You probably won't today," Kelvin said, pointing to the schedule. "The eighth graders are tough."

Theresa looked at the eighth-grade girls' schedule. "Somebody beat them, so they can be beat," she said with a sniff.

"Come on, Theresa," Nikki said. "We gotta warm up." Theresa, Nikki, and the rest of the girls' team raced out onto the floor. The crowd of students and parents that filled the gymnasium for the yearly game burst into cheers. The four boys walked into the gym behind the girls' team.

"Hey, there's T. J. and Bobby," Conor said, pointing to the stands. "Let's go sit with them."

The boys traded high fives as they settled into their seats. Kelvin and Michael stood up and started chanting and clapping.

"'Somebody beat them, so they can be beat,'
Theresa said with a sniff."

"Let's go, seventh grade. Let's go."

"Let's go, seventh grade. Let's go."

When the chant died down, James Becker yelled through cupped hands from a few rows away.

"Yeah, maybe your grade will win one game this year," he teased. "The girls' game."

"We'll see you guys tomorrow," Kelvin called back.

"If you guys show up," Jerome Dobson answered with a laugh.

"We'll be there!" Kelvin yelled back bravely and then sat down. "We may get beat," he whispered to his friends. "But we'll be there."

The boys shared a laugh and turned their attention to the game. The seventh-grade girls battled hard to keep it close. Theresa and Nikki hit long shots near the end of the half to cut the eighth-grade lead to two points, 16–14.

At halftime, Michael and his friends led the cheers for the seventh-grade girls.

"Two bits, four bits, six bits, a dollar, all for the seventh grade stand up and holler!"

But the boys' cheers were not enough. The eighth-grade girls pulled away in the second half. When the buzzer sounded, the eighth grade had won again, 35–26.

Michael stepped down from the stands and

joined the crowd of players, students, and parents milling around the court after the game.

"Hey, Theresa, good game," he said to his disappointed friend. "You almost had them."

"They were too good for us," Theresa said, shaking her head. Her brown hair was matted with sweat. She took one more tired look at the scoreboard. "They were just too good, too big, and too old," she said.

TWELVE

Michael took the key from his pocket, slipped it into the Mancinos' back door, and went inside. The house was quiet and still. He spied a note on the kitchen table.

Daniel and Michael—

I've gone to show the Papas' house. I should be back by 6:30. There are leftovers in the fridge.

Love, Mom

"Daniel," Michael called. No answer.

Michael opened up the refrigerator and took a swig of juice from an open carton, put it back, and closed the door. He grabbed a basketball from among several that were piled in a plastic laundry basket in the corner of the kitchen and stepped outside.

The early spring sun was setting behind the houses, turning the sky into brilliant streaks of pink and red. As Michael practiced his shots in the empty driveway, his mind wandered to the next day's game with the eighth graders. He stood at a line scratched in the driveway, fifteen feet from the basket.

If I hit this foul shot, he told himself, *the seventh-grade boys will beat the eighth-grade boys for the first time in school history.*

Michael bounced the ball three times. *Thump, thump, thump.* He took a deep breath and sent the ball up toward the basket. The ball hit the back of the rim and bounced straight back. Michael grabbed the ball and set up for another free throw. *Okay,* he thought, determined, *if I hit this foul shot, the seventh grade wins.* This time, the ball sailed straight and true. The net danced in the fading sunlight.

"Hey, I'm open," Daniel called from the end of the driveway. Michael turned, smiled, and passed the ball to his brother. The boys started moving about the driveway, trading shots and passes as they talked.

"How did the girls' game go?"

"The seventh grade lost, 35–26."

"That's pretty close. How'd Theresa do?"

"She scored around ten. Are you gonna be at the scorer's table for our game tomorrow?"

"Yeah. Think you guys got a chance to win?"

"Our full-court press gives us a chance."

"Yeah, I guess. What about that big kid from Nigeria? What's his name?"

"Dikembe Obiku."

"That's a weird name. How do you spell it?"

"D-I-K-E-M-B-E O-B-I-K-U."

"Well, what about him?" Daniel continued. "Is he gonna play tomorrow? You know you don't have to be on the team to play in the seventh- and eighth-grade game."

"Yeah, I know. But he's got some family party or something he has to go to," Michael answered as he passed the ball to Daniel. "I hope he can still make it."

Daniel tossed up a high jump shot. *Swish.*

"Give me another, Michael," Daniel said, his hands open to the ball. Michael kept passing and Daniel kept shooting, making basket after basket. Daniel became more excited with every basket that ripped through the net.

"I can't miss!"

Swish.

"The man is on fire!"

Swish.

Michael followed the next pass out to Daniel.

"Let's see you make one with somebody guarding you," he challenged his older brother.

"Okay." Daniel grinned. "I guess your big brother will have to teach you to respect your elders."

Daniel spun quickly and sent up a jump shot over Michael's tight defense. The ball bounced off the rim and Michael snared the rebound.

Michael dribbled to the end of the driveway, turned to face the basket, and looked straight at Daniel.

"Come on," he said. "One on one. Game to seven. House championship."

"Okay, little brother." Daniel smiled. "But no whining when I beat you. Your ball."

Michael dribbled quickly to the left to start the game, stopped, and put up a fadeaway jump shot. Sensing the shot was too long, Michael quickly followed the ball to the basket. He grabbed the rebound and laid the ball up and in for the first basket.

1–0.

Michael faked a long shot and drove hard to the right. He flipped a running right-hander over his brother that banked off the backboard and in.

2–0.

Michael then stretched his lead to 3–0 with a scoop shot under Daniel's arm that spun off the edge of the backboard and through the net.

"Nice shot," Daniel admitted.

"Sorry, that was disrespectful," Michael said cheerily.

"Game's to seven," Daniel said as he flipped the ball to Michael. "You only got three."

"Gotta win by two?" Michael asked.

Daniel shook his head. "Nah, straight sevens. First guy with seven baskets wins."

Michael faked right and drove left and tried another fadeaway jumper. The ball glanced off the rim and Daniel grabbed the rebound.

"I think it's time to get my respect, little brother," he said as he dribbled back. Daniel stopped for a long jump shot.

Swish. 3–1.

The brothers continued to battle as evening fell. Two lights at the Mancinos' back door cast a dim yellow glow on the driveway and the two boys playing there. Michael tossed up a twisting jumper that bounced around the rim and in.

"6–5, my lead," Michael said, standing twenty feet from the basket with his hands out, his breath heavy with effort. "Straight sevens, right?" he asked.

Daniel nodded, bent at the waist with his hands on his knees. Michael grabbed the ball and the boys snapped into action.

Michael dribbled right and tried his best running right-handed shot, but it was just a touch too hard. The ball bounced off the backboard, teetered on the edge of the rim, and rolled off.

Daniel grabbed the rebound, dribbled back, and drove hard to the hoop. Michael reached high, hoping to block his shot.

"Foul. My ball," Daniel called.

"Foul?" Michael cried. "I barely touched you."

"You got my wrist."

"That's a wimp call."

"My call, my ball," Daniel said fiercely. Then he took the ball, faked a quick move, and feathered a long shot to the hoop.

Swish.

6–6.

"Next basket wins," Daniel said. He spun the ball between his hands. "House championship."

Michael's eyes narrowed. He took a deep breath through his nose.

"Next basket wins," he repeated. "House championship."

Daniel drove left and stopped for his favorite

fadeaway jump shot. Knowing he had no chance to block his big brother's shot, Michael rushed toward the basket, hoping for a rebound.

The ball knocked off the back of the basket, touched the backboard, and then wobbled on the edge of the rim. As Michael looked up helplessly, the ball finally fell through the net.

"Yes!" Daniel shouted, punching the air with both fists. "Better luck tomorrow," he called as he dashed into the house. "But your big brother is just too good for you."

Michael stood under the basket in the chilled quiet of the gathering night. He slammed the basketball into the driveway with both hands.

Too good, he thought. *Too good, too big, too old.*

THIRTEEN

The cheers of the packed crowd greeted the seventh-grade Falcons as they ran out onto the court for warm-ups.

"Man, look at the crowd," Conor whispered to Michael in the layup line. "It's big."

Michael nodded nervously as he looked around. Michael's mother sat in the last row among some of the other parents. Daniel stood at the scorer's table, watching the seconds click down before the start of the seventh-and-eighth-grade-boys basketball game.

When the last second ticked away, Daniel sounded the horn and the teams huddled around their coaches. Coach Cummings shouted above the noise in the gym.

"All right, guys, we gotta play hard and smart. We're in better shape than they are, so the press will wear them down. Same starters. Martin and T. J. at guards. Michael, Charlie, and Conor in the frontcourt."

Coach Cummings put his hand out. The players piled their hands on his. "You can beat these guys," Coach Cummings said.

"DEE-fense!" the Falcons team shouted. The starters ran onto the court.

As the teams' starters shook hands, Michael noticed that each eighth-grade starter was several inches taller than the seventh graders. *Just like the UCLA-Michigan game,* Michael thought. *I hope we can win just like the Bruins.*

The referee tossed the ball up and the battle began. The eighth grade controlled the tap and passed the ball around the seventh grade's swarming defense. James Becker, the eighth-grade center, caught a quick pass inside and was about to score when Charlie Rosenthal knocked the ball out of bounds.

"Blue ball," the referee called.

"Stack it up!" Jerome Dobson shouted. The eighth graders stood in a straight line to the left side of the basket.

"Break!" Jerome called.

All the players except James scattered. Jerome lofted the ball to James, who caught it and laid it in off the backboard for an easy basket.

As Michael ran downcourt, Jerome smiled and teased, "That was easy."

But Michael and his teammates did not give up easily. The two teams battled back and forth. The eighth-grade players used their height and strength to muscle close to the basket for easy scores. The seventh-grade players used their quickness and full-court press to steal passes and race down the floor for layups. The first half ended with the eighth grade clinging to a 21−18 lead.

During halftime, the seventh-grade Falcons shot practice shots from a semicircle around the basket. Gina rebounded underneath.

"Come on, we're in this one!" Michael yelled to his teammates.

"We can beat 'em!" Conor agreed. "Let's keep it up."

"I still wish we had a big guy," Kelvin said, practicing a foul shot.

"Shut up!" Conor snapped. "We can beat them without one. The press will beat them."

"You guys are doing great," Gina encouraged the team as she passed the ball to Michael.

Michael swished a long jump shot just as the horn sounded for the beginning of the second half. *Maybe that's a good sign,* he thought.

The second half settled into a familiar pattern. The eighth grade scored whenever they could get the ball close to their basket. But the seventh grade's full-court press created just enough turn-overs and steals to keep the game close.

As the fourth quarter wound down, Michael came out of the game. He took a long gulp of water and a seat on the bench. Then he looked at the scoreboard. Down by five.

"Come on, seventh grade!" he shouted. "Need a hoop."

Just then, Dikembe, dressed in sneakers, jeans, and a white seventh-grade practice jersey, slipped onto the end of the bench.

"How are we doing?" he asked Michael.

"Hey, you made it," Michael said, surprised to see his friend. "We're only down by five, with about three minutes to go. I don't think the coach will put you in the game this close to the end."

"That's okay," Dikembe said. "I just want to see us win."

Dikembe stood up at the end of the bench and shouted, "Come on, seventh grade! Need a hoop."

T. J. dribbled the ball down the left side of the court. The eighth-grade defense surrounded the little guard. T. J. flipped a quick pass to Charlie Rosenthal, the seventh-grade center, who was standing two feet beyond the three-point line.

Charlie looked from side to side, trying to find a teammate to pass the ball to. Finally Charlie lofted a long one-hand push shot toward the basket.

"No!" cried Michael from the bench as the ball sailed toward the basket.

Swish!

"Yes!" Michael cried, jumping up and down in front of the bench. "Three-pointer!"

"Bruin!"

The eighth grade tried a long pass downcourt. But Kelvin intercepted and passed to Conor for a wide-open three-pointer.

Swish!

In a matter of seconds, the seventh grade had grabbed the lead: 39–38!

"Time-out!" Mr. Pickman, the eight graders' coach, called from the stunned eighth-grade bench. "Time-out," he said again as he kept stabbing the palm of one hand with the fingertips of his other hand to form a *T*.

The seventh-grade bench was a mob scene. The whole team, along with Gina and Dikembe, were pounding Conor on the back.

"All right, Conor!"

"Clutch hoop!"

Coach Cummings's voice cut through the huddle's happy chaos.

"Listen up!" he shouted. He began barking instructions. "There's over a minute left. Michael, check back in for Bobby. Gina, how many time-outs does each team have left?"

The coach's voice seemed to settle the seventh graders. Coach Cummings looked around the suddenly silent huddle. "This game is not over yet," he warned. "Let's keep the pressure on."

The coach was right. The eighth graders moved the ball slowly downcourt and worked the ball to James Becker. The tall center faked left and tossed up a soft hook shot.

The shot was good! The eighth graders had grabbed back the lead, 40–39.

The seventh graders rushed downcourt, trying to beat the clock that was winding down. Charlie snapped a pass out to Conor, who was standing beyond the three-point line. Conor looked ready to try the long shot, but at the last instant, Michael cut to the basket. Conor drilled a pass to Michael, who scored on a twisting layup. The seventh grade led, 41–40!

"Bruin!"

The seventh graders instantly set up the press. Michael stretched and deflected a bounce pass. The ball bounced wildly to the left. Michael darted over, grabbed the spinning ball, and started dribbling, hoping to run out the clock.

Jerome Dobson chased Michael, slapping wildly at the ball.

Phweeeet! the whistle shrieked.

"Foul. Blue 25," the referee called, pointing to Jerome. "White ball."

The horn sounded. Daniel sat at the scorer's table, waving the index finger of each hand high above his head. "One and one," he called.

One and one, Michael thought, just beginning to panic. *I'm going to shoot foul shots to win the game!*

FOURTEEN

Michael could barely feel his feet as he walked to the foul line.

His mind raced over the game situation. *Twelve seconds to go. We're up by one, 41–40. I'm shooting one and one. If I make the first foul shot, I get a chance for another. If I miss, the eighth grade will probably get a shot at winning the game.*

Michael felt his heart pound and his fingertips tingle as the referee held the ball out to him.

"One and one. The ball's live," the referee said. "Hold your positions until he releases the ball."

Michael wiped his damp palms against his shirt before taking the ball. He spread his feet out behind the foul line and bounced the ball three times. *Thump, thump, thump.* He took a deep breath and focused on the front edge of the rim.

Just like last night, he thought. *The second shot last night.*

The moment he shot the ball, Michael sensed it was not high enough.

"Short!" he screamed.

The ball bounced off the front rim. James Becker snatched the rebound with two hands and passed to Jake McClure.

Michael, disappointed, scrambled down the court, racing to get back on defense.

Jake dribbled down the right side of the court as the crowd counted down the final seconds.

"Ten...nine...eight..."

Michael saw a blue-shirted eighth grader streaking to the basket a few steps ahead of him. Jake also spied his teammate and flicked a quick bounce pass to him. Michael dove forward, tapped the ball away with his fingertips, and skidded across the polished floor on his chest.

"Blue ball!" the referee called.

"Time-out. Time-out!" Mr. Pickman cried, waving his hands in front of the eighth-grade bench.

Michael picked himself off the floor and looked at the clock. Four seconds to go. Coach Cummings was off the bench.

"Great hustle, Michael," he said. He pointed out to the floor. "Gina, ask the referee where the eighth grade will take the ball out."

Gina returned in a flash. "Left side of the basket, right underneath," she said excitedly. "They'll try that play they used the first quarter where they pass to James Becker for an easy layup."

Kelvin groaned. "Man, we don't have anyone tall enough to cover Becker," he said.

"How about Dikembe?" Michael said, pointing to the towering seventh grader standing at the edge of the team huddle.

"When did you get here?" Coach Cummings asked.

"A couple of minutes ago," Michael blurted out. "He's tall enough to cover Becker."

"You got sneakers on?" the coach asked.

Dikembe's face lit up. "Yes," he said, pointing to his feet.

"Okay," Coach Cummings decided. "Dikembe, report in for Charlie."

Dressed in his white practice T-shirt and jeans, Dikembe started to the scorer's table.

Mr. Pickman stopped him before he reached the table. "Hey, he can't play," Mr. Pickman said, looking straight at the referee. "He's not on the team."

Coach Cummings stepped out onto the floor. "The game is the seventh-grade boys against the eighth-grade boys," he explained. "He is a seventh-grade boy."

The referee stood between the coaches, a bit confused. "Well..." the referee started, scratching his head.

"He may be a seventh grader," Mr. Pickman protested, "but he can't play because he's not listed in the official score book."

The referee walked over to the scorer's table. Coach Cummings turned to Michael with a pained look. "I didn't put his name in the book," Coach Cummings whispered to Michael.

"What's his name?" the referee asked, looking down at the score book.

"Dikembe Obiku," Coach Cummings said, with a hint of despair in his voice. "O-B-I-K-U."

"He's here. He's in the score book," the referee declared. "Come on, let's play ball."

Michael's jaw dropped and he stared wide-eyed at Daniel sitting at the scorer's table.

Coach Cummings didn't waste any time. "Everybody get a man!" he yelled as the Falcons ran back out onto the floor. "Dikembe, you take Becker. Number fifteen."

The eighth graders lined up in a straight row to the left of the basket. Jerome Dobson held the ball and called "Break!"

Just as at the beginning of the game, all the eighth graders scattered except for James Becker. Jerome lofted a high pass toward James. But Dikembe jumped with him, his right hand tapping the ball to the corner.

Michael raced over and caught the loose ball. He flung it high into the air. The buzzer sounded before the ball hit the floor.

The seventh grade had won!

The team surrounded Coach Cummings and Dikembe in a wild backslapping celebration. In the middle of the happy circle, Kelvin tossed his head back and screamed above the noise, "I told you we needed a big guy!"

After the teams shook hands and the crowd drifted away, Michael stood at the center of the floor, still in his uniform. He did not want to leave the magic of the moment.

"Come on, Michael," Daniel called from the doorway at the corner of the gym. "Mom's getting the car." Michael walked slowly across the floor and stood next to Daniel.

"How come Dikembe's name was in the score book?" he asked, looking up at his big brother.

A small smile creased Daniel's face. "I figured it was about time the younger guys got a

*"But Dikembe jumped with him, his right hand
tapping the ball to the corner."*

chance to win one," he said. "Come on, Mom's waiting."

Michael took one last look at the gym. The stands were empty now. The scoreboard was blank. The school janitor pushed a wide mop silently across the gym floor.

41–40, Michael remembered with silent satisfaction. Then he turned and walked outside.

"Yes!" he screamed at the top of his lungs to the silent winter sky.

FIFTEEN

The next day, Michael stretched out on the warm grass next to the basketball court at Hobbs Park, propping up his head with a basketball for a pillow. The sun of a suddenly springlike Saturday afternoon warmed him.

On the court, Conor, Kelvin, Charlie, and Dikembe shot baskets lazily in the bright sunshine. After a while, Conor and Kelvin joined Michael on the grass. They sat with their legs stretched out and their backs against the brick school building.

"Hey, where's T. J. and Bobby?" Kelvin asked, looking around the park. "I thought they were coming down to play some hoop."

Conor shook his head. "Nah, T. J. said they were gonna go down to Green Street to play baseball."

Michael shielded his eyes against the sun. "It still feels too early for baseball," he said.

"Where are the eighth graders?" Kelvin asked

with a chuckle, still looking around the park. "I guess they went up to the high school to get some tougher competition."

The boys all laughed, remembering the previous day's upset.

"You know, I was just thinking about the game," Michael said, pulling himself up.

"So what," Kelvin laughed. "That's all any of us have been thinking or talking about since yesterday."

Michael sat between his two friends, his back pressed against the warm bricks of the school building.

"No, really," he continued, "I was thinking, you know who won that game for us?"

"Dikembe," Conor answered. "He tipped the ball away from Becker."

"Nope," Michael said, shaking his head.

"Your brother," Kelvin said. "He put Dikembe's name in the score book."

"No. My Uncle Dave."

"Who?" Conor and Kelvin said together.

"My Uncle Dave," Michael repeated. "You remember? He gave me that $15 gift certificate to the House of Cards. Without that, we never would have known about the UCLA full-court press."

"Bruin!" Kelvin shouted, throwing his hands

in the air and laughing.

Conor took a long breath of spring air. "You know, you're right," he said. "The full-court press really saved us."

"Hey, what happened to UCLA after that?" Kelvin asked. "Did they win the NCAA tournament again?"

"Oh yeah," Michael said. "The year after the two years that they won the NCAAs with the press, they didn't even get in the tournament. Then they won the NCAAs eight of the next nine years."

"Wow!" Conor exclaimed. "Did they use the press?"

Michael nodded and placed a long blade of grass between his teeth. "They still used the press sometimes," he said. "But also they recruited some big guys."

"Like who?" Kelvin asked.

"Well, the year after they didn't make the tournament, they got Lew Alcindor."

Kelvin looked surprised. "Lew Alcindor? I've never heard of him."

"He changed his name after college to Kareem Abdul-Jabbar."

"They got Kareem!" Conor shouted. "Man, he was the best."

The three boys looked at the basketball court where Dikembe and Charlie were playing one-on-one. Just then Dikembe faked left, turned right, and flipped a graceful hook shot to the basket. As the ball swished softly through the net, the three friends shared the same thought.

Michael looked at Conor, then at Kelvin, and smiled.

"I think we're gonna be *really* good next year," he said.

The End

But read on—
there's more…

The UCLA Bruins
The Real Story

EARLY IN THE FIRST HALF of the 1964 National Collegiate Athletic Association (NCAA) championship game, the University of California at Los Angeles (UCLA) Bruins were trailing the Duke Blue Devils. The Bruins coach, John Wooden, could see his team losing control, so he did something he almost never did: He called time-out early in the game.

Wooden sat his nervous team down. He told his players not to lose confidence in themselves or the full-court pressing defense. Remember, stay with press and always have two Bruins covering the Blue Devil who has the ball, he told them.

Wooden knew that the press would force the Blue Devils to make bad passes and speed up the game. The Bruins were the quicker team, so they would have an advantage in a fast-paced game.

Wooden also figured the press would wear the Blue Devils down, and he was right. Within a few minutes, the Bruins had cut the Blue Devils lead to three points, 30–27. Then the Bruins press really got rolling. In the next 2 minutes and 40 seconds, the Bruins scored 16 points and the Blue Devils scored none. The final score of the game was 98–83. The UCLA Bruins and John Wooden had won their first NCAA championship!

It would not be their last. In the twelve seasons from 1964 through 1975, Wooden's UCLA Bruins won an amazing ten NCAA championships. No college coach or team has ever come close to matching that winning streak.

Coach John Wooden

John Wooden may be the greatest coach in the history of college basketball. He was successful with many different teams and players. Some of his championship teams were led by such legendary big men as Kareem Abdul-Jabbar and Bill Walton. But Wooden's first NCAA championship team, the team that beat the Duke Blue Devils and were 30-0 for the 1963–64 season, had no big men. In fact, the Bruins did not have a single starter that season who was over 6 feet 5 inches tall. (That's an inch shorter than Michael Jordan!) But the Bruins made up for their lack of height with speed, hustle, and the full-court zone press, designed by Coach Wooden.

Like lots of coaches, John Wooden first learned about basketball by playing basketball. Wooden was a star in high school who went on to be a three-time all-American at Purdue University from 1930 to 1932. Wooden was such a great player that he is the only person inducted into the National Basketball Hall of Fame in Springfield, Massachusetts, as both a player *and* a coach.

Wooden first learned about the idea of a full-court defense from his coach at Purdue, Ward "Piggy" Lambert. After Purdue, Wooden played semipro basketball on the weekends to make extra money, but did not play in a professional basketball league as college stars do today. The National Basketball Association, the NBA, did not start until years later, in 1946. Instead, Wooden coached high school basketball (and taught high school English). His teams' record over eleven years was 218 wins and only 42 losses.

Wooden moved on to coach college basketball, first at Indiana State and then at UCLA. Each of Wooden's teams used the full-court zone press in certain situations, but never for an entire game. That changed in the 1963–64 season, when Wooden decided to use the full-court press all the time. That season, the Bruins' full-court press blew away opposing teams. The fast-breaking Bruins went undefeated and won all but seven of their thirty games by ten points or more.

Wooden didn't have any big men that season, but he had players who were perfect for the press. Walt Hazzard and Gail Goodrich were a pair of all-American ball-hawking guards, and Keith Erickson was a quick-thinking forward who played the last line of defense in the press. Erickson had an uncanny sense of when to move up for a steal and when to stay back and guard the basket.

The next season (1964–65), the Bruins were still not big, and they kept the full-court pressure on. Despite a pair of early-season losses, UCLA streaked through the NCAA tournament averaging 100 points a game and defeating the favored and much bigger University of Michigan Wolverines 91–80. In the championship game, Gail Goodrich, the smallest player on the court, led UCLA to victory with 42 points.

Gail Goodrich, Walt Hazzard, and Keith Erickson went on to have long NBA careers, and Gail Goodrich made it into the National Basketball Hall of Fame.

UCLA Bruins 1963-64
NCAA championship team

There were more championships to come after the 1964–65 season. But with their first two championship victories, John Wooden and the UCLA Bruins proved you do not have to *be* big to *play* big. You just need to have good players, a lot of heart, and the willingness to go full-court.

Acknowledgments

The author would like to thank Mr. Bill Bennett, the Associate Sports Information Director at UCLA, for providing information on the UCLA basketball program and especially the championship teams of 1964 and 1965. Much of the information about John Wooden and the UCLA championship teams in The Real Story chapter is from John Wooden's book THEY CALL ME COACH.

ALLSTAR SPORTSTORY BOOKS BY FRED BOWEN

ON THE LINE • 1-56145-199-1
Marcus is the highest scorer and best rebounder on his junior high school basketball team, but he's not so great at free throws. Mr. Dunn, the school custodian, helps him face and overcome his fear of failure.

OFF THE RIM • 1-56145-161-4
Chris yearns to be more than a benchwarmer on the Oak View Middle School basketball team. With the help of his best friend Greta and her mom, Chris begins to change his defensive strategy and successfully learns to keep his opponents from scoring.

THE FINAL CUT • 1-56145-192-4
Ryan, Zeke, Eli, and Miles are four close friends who share a love of sports, especially basketball. But now they are in seventh grade and have to go through tryouts in order to make the school basketball team. Slowly it becomes clear that they may not all make the team, and that the tryouts are a test not only of their athletic skills, but also of their friendship.

FULL COURT FEVER • 1-56145-160-6
The Falcons have a problem: they have the skill but not the height required to win their games. An old issue of Sports Illustrated reveals the story of the UCLA Bruins, who used the full court zone press to compensate for a roster of short players. Will the Falcons be able to make a comeback and win the dreaded end-of-the- season game against their much taller eighth-grade rivals?

T.J.'S SECRET PITCH • 1-56145-119-3
T.J. loves baseball, and hopes to pitch for his team. But he's smaller than his teammates and his pitches just don't have the power to get the batters out. When he learns about 1940s baseball star Rip Sewell and his mysterious pitch, he may have found a solution.

THE GOLDEN GLOVE • 1-56145-133-9
Without his lucky glove, Jamie doesn't believe in his ability to lead his baseball team to victory. Then he learns that faith in oneself is the most important equipment for any game. Includes the fascinating history of baseball gloves with player profiles and lots of baseball facts.

THE KID COACH • 1-56145-140-1
Scott and his teammates can't find an adult to coach the team, so they must find a leader among themselves. Woven into the story are real-life tales of player-managers in the Major Leagues.

PLAYOFF DREAMS • 1-56145-155-X
Brendan is one of the best players in the league, but no matter how hard he tries, he can't make his team win. An un-expected event and the story of legendary Cubs player and Hall of Fame member Ernie Banks make Brendan realize that it's the love of the game rather than winning that makes the experience a success.

WINNERS TAKE ALL • 1-56145-229-7
Kyle claims to have made a difficult catch, which he actually dropped. But the heady excitement of the praise and attention he receives is not enough to silence his conscience.

About the Author

One of the biggest disappointments of Fred Bowen's life was that he did not make his high school varsity basketball team in Marblehead, Massachusetts. But he did not stop playing. Mr. Bowen played pickup basketball and in recreational leagues for twenty-five years. He played on one team, the Court Jesters, for eighteen straight seasons.

Over a period of thirteen years, Mr. Bowen coached thirty-one different kid's sports teams in soccer, baseball, softball, and basketball

Mr. Bowen, author of T.J.'s SECRET PITCH, THE GOLDEN GLOVE, THE KID COACH, PLAYOFF DREAMS, WINNERS TAKE ALL, ON THE LINE, OFF THE RIM, THE FINAL CUT AND FULL COURT FEVER lives in Silver Spring, Maryland, with his wife and two children.

Book Six in the
AllStar SportStory Series—

OFF THE RIM

Chris wants to be a star on the
boys' basketball team, but almost all
his shots bounce off the rim.

When Chris asks Greta, the super-
star of the girls' team, for help, he
learns that teams need more than
shooting stars to win.

Look for Fred Bowen's
OFF THE RIM